To cheese lovers everywhere!

BLOOMSBURY CHILDREN'S BOOKS
Bloomsbury Publishing Inc., part of Bloomsbury Publishing Plc
1359 Broadway, New York, NY 10018
50 Bedford Square, London, WC1B 3DP, UK
Bloomsbury Publishing Ireland Limited, 29 Earlsfort Terrace, Dublin 2, D02 AY28, Ireland

BLOOMSBURY, BLOOMSBURY CHILDREN'S BOOKS, and the Diana logo are trademarks of Bloomsbury Publishing Plc

First published in the United States of America in September 2025
by Bloomsbury Children's Books

Text and illustrations copyright © 2025 by Salina Yoon

All rights reserved. No part of this publication may be: i) reproduced or transmitted in any form, electronic or mechanical, including photocopying, recording, or by means of any information storage or retrieval system without prior permission in writing from the publishers; or ii) used or reproduced in any way for the training, development, or operation of artificial intelligence (AI) technologies, including generative AI technologies. The rights holders expressly reserve this publication from the text and data mining exception as per Article 4(3) of the Digital Single Market Directive (EU) 2019/790.

Bloomsbury books may be purchased for business or promotional use. For information on bulk purchases please contact Macmillan Corporate and Premium Sales Department at specialmarkets@macmillan.com

Library of Congress Cataloging-in-Publication Data
available upon request
ISBN 978-1-5476-1242-0 (hardcover) • ISBN 978-1-5476-1243-7 (e-book) • ISBN 978-1-5476-1244-4 (e-PDF)

Art created digitally using Adobe Photoshop
Typeset in Londrina Solid
Book design by Salina Yoon and Yelena Safronova
Printed in China by Leo Paper Products, Heshan, Guangdong
2 4 6 8 10 9 7 5 3 1

To find out more about our authors and books visit www.bloomsbury.com and sign up for our newsletters.
For product safety-related questions contact productsafety@bloomsbury.com.

A Kat & Mouse Book

I Like CHEESE!

Salina Yoon

BLOOMSBURY
CHILDREN'S BOOKS
NEW YORK LONDON OXFORD NEW DELHI SYDNEY

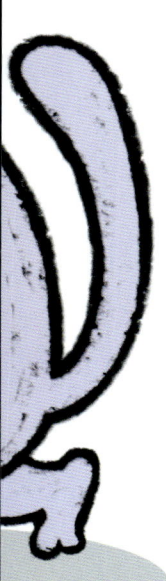

THE NEXT DAY

"What's for lunch today, Kat?"

... salami, ham, lettuce, tomato, onions,

I made a spectacular sandwich with . . .

and pickles—inside a freshly baked roll.

I call it . . .

THE NEXT DAY

THE DAY AFTER THAT

AND THE DAY AFTER THAT

YES! But it's okay to try new things, too. AND new lunches!

I packed something different for BOTH of us to try!

I like cheese, and you like sandwiches, so I made something special just for us.

Did you bring a NEW lunch, Mouse?!

I call it . . .